BEST-LOVED
IRISH
LEGENDS

EITHNE MASSEY
ILLUSTRATED BY LISA JACKSON

THE O'BRIEN PRESS
DUBLIN

Eithne Massey is a graduate of UCD and NUI Maynooth, and her interest in mythology is a lifelong one. She lives between Ireland and Brittany. Her other books are: *The Secret of Kells, The Dreaming Tree, The Silver Stag of Bunratty, Where the Stones Sing* and *Blood Brother, Swan Sister* and *Legendary Ireland*.

Lisa Jackson was born in Dublin and grew up in north Co. Wicklow. She studied classical animation for four years at Senior College Ballyfermot, then worked in animation, graphic design and comic books. Lisa now illustrates children's books.

CONTENTS

THE SALMON OF KNOWLEDG

PRONUNCIATION GUIDE
Fionn: *fyun*; Finnegas: *finnayguss*

Long ago, there lived a boy called Fionn, who wanted to know everything. His mother got tired of answering his questions, so she sent him to live with two wise women. They taught Fionn many things. Then, one day, they too got tired of answering his questions. They sent him to live with the wisest man in Ireland, who was called Finnegas. But even he did not know everything. And even he got tired of being asked questions by Fionn.

'How can I know everything?' asked Fionn.
'Everything in the whole world?'
'I'm not going to tell you that,' said Finnegas.
(Finnegas had a secret.)

Fionn did all the jobs around the house for
Finnegas. He didn't like the cooking and
cleaning, but he loved the hunting and fishing.
Finnegas often sent him to fish in a pool in the
river Boyne. Fionn liked it there because he
could sit in the shade of a huge old hazel tree.
He would watch the hazel nuts fall into the
water and drift away. Sometimes a silver salmon
came up from the depths of the pool and
swallowed the nuts.

Then one day, Fionn caught the salmon.
When Finnegas saw the fish, he became very
excited. 'Cook it at once,' he said, 'and don't eat
a single bit of it. This fish is all for me.'
Fionn thought this was a bit unfair. The salmon
was huge, and *he* was the one who had caught it.
But Finnegas was his master,
so he would do as he was told.

He lit a fire and cooked the salmon. Even though it smelt
delicious, he did not taste any of it. But as he was taking it
off the fire, he burnt his thumb on the salmon's hot,
bubbling skin. He stuck his thumb in his mouth and sucked
it to stop the pain. Then he took the fish to Finnegas.
'You didn't eat any of the salmon, did you?' Finnegas asked
suspiciously, his voice squeaking with worry.

'I did not,' said Fionn.

'You didn't even taste its skin, did you?' said Finnegas.
Fionn started to say, I did not, again. Then he remembered.
'I just put my finger in my mouth when I burnt it on the
skin,' he said. 'But I didn't eat any.'

egas was furious. 'Now *you* have it! *You* have the knowledge!'
he roared. 'What?' said Fionn. 'What are you saying?'

'That fish is the Salmon of Knowledge,' said Finnegas.
'It has eaten the nuts from the ancient hazel tree that holds
ll the knowledge in the world. And the first person to taste
that salmon gains all the wisdom there is!'

nn was amazed. 'You can have the rest of it,' he said guiltily.
s no use now,' said Finnegas. 'It's only a stupid, ordinary fish.
Now all its knowledge is inside you.'

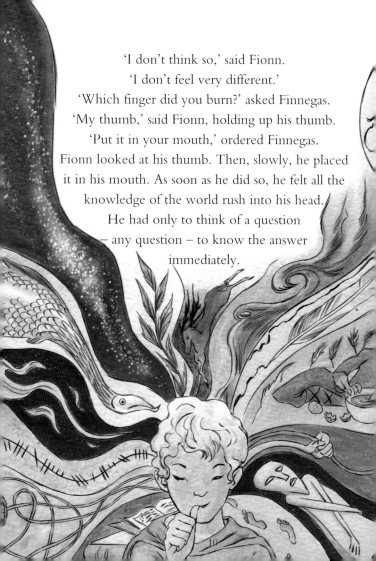

'I don't think so,' said Fionn.
'I don't feel very different.'
'Which finger did you burn?' asked Finnegas.
'My thumb,' said Fionn, holding up his thumb.
'Put it in your mouth,' ordered Finnegas.
Fionn looked at his thumb. Then, slowly, he placed
it in his mouth. As soon as he did so, he felt all the
knowledge of the world rush into his head.
He had only to think of a question
– any question – to know the answer
immediately.

10

Poor Finnegas! They ate the rest of the fish together anyway. But Finnegas could not eat very much. He knew now he would never have the wisdom he had waited for all his life.

Instead, the knowledge had gone to a little boy.

When Fionn grew up, he became a great warrior and hunter, and a wise leader of the Fianna, the greatest band of warriors Ireland has ever known. And whenever he needed to know something – anything – all he had to do was put his thumb in his mouth and bite hard on it.

He never had to ask anyone any questions, ever again.

HOW CÚ CHULAINN GOT HIS NAME

Culann was the smith of King Conor, and he had a savage guard dog. It was called the Cú, or the 'Hound'. It bit people first and worried about it later. It was so savage that people said it ate puppies for breakfast!

The Cú was kept in an iron cage, and only let out to roam around the smith's house when everyone was safely locked inside. But Culann's house was never attacked or robbed, because everyone knew about the Cú.

One day, King Conor came to feast with Culann, and when everyone was safely inside, the Cú was let out to protect the house from the king's enemies.

But Conor had forgotten something. His nephew, Setanta, had been playing hurling when Conor left the palace to go to Culann's house. Conor had told the boy to follow him to the feast when the game was finished.

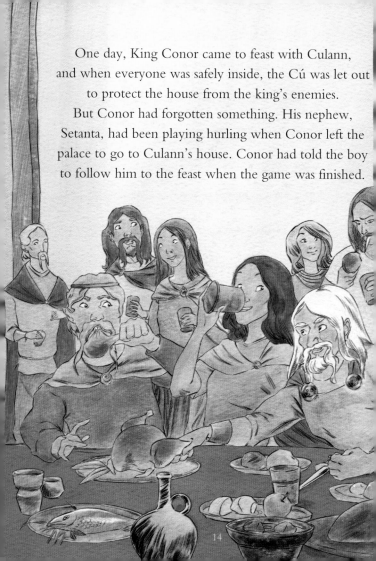

An hour later, Setanta came along the road, whistling. He was only seven, but he was already the best hurler in Ireland. Now he practised hitting the *sliotar* high into the air as he walked along.

But wait! Something was patrolling the walls of Culann's hou
It lifted its head and slobbered horribly, sniffing fresh young b
Setanta came to the gate. He saw a large black shadow. He
heard an enormous growl. Something huge and hairy was fly
through the air towards him! He caught a glimpse of long
yellow fangs and dripping jaws. Of red eyes.

Without even stopping to think, Setanta let the
ball fly. It was a wonderful shot. It whizzed like
lightning through the air – and went straight
down the monster's throat. The dog leapt high
in agony, then dropped to the ground, dead.

Setanta went up to it cautiously. 'They welcome strangers strangely here,' he said. 'Who are you?' asked a deep voice and there was Culann, with Conor and all his court, staring at the fallen dog. They had heard the noise and come rushing out. King Conor was white with fear. He had finally remembered that Setanta was on his way to the 'I was nearly killed by that dog,' said Setanta. 'I am Setanta King Conor's nephew. I came to his court to train as a Red Branch Knight.' The Red Branch Knights were the king's warriors. 'And you will be a great one,' said King Conor proudly. He was smiling now. 'No one else could have killed the Cú.'

'That's all very well,' said Culann.
'But I have lost the best guard dog in Ireland.
What will I do now?' Setanta thought for a minute.
vill guard your house in exchange for having killed the Cú,'
ated. 'I will protect you from harm until a puppy is raised to
take the place of the dog you lost.'
So it was agreed. And Culann's house was never attacked
or robbed as long as Setanta was guarding it. And,
n when Setanta became the most famous warrior in Ireland,
he was not called Setanta, but 'Culann's Hound',
or Cú Chulainn.

THE **CHILDREN** OF **LIR**

PRONUNCIATION GUIDE
Fionnuala: *finnoola*; Aodh: *a*
Fiachra: *feeakrah*; Conn: *con*; Aoife: *eef*

20

Fionnuala was a princess. She had three brothers, Aodh, Fiachra and Conn. Fiachra and Conn were twins, and as wild as hares. The only time they were still was at the end of the day, when their mother sang them to sleep. But the queen died and everyone was very sad for a long time. Then King Lir married again. Aoife, his new wife, was very beautiful. But what no one knew was that she was a witch. She was jealous of Lir's love for his children and came to hate them. She especially hated it when Fionnuala sang her mother's songs to Conn and Fiachra, because she herself had a voice like a crow. One day, she said to Fionnuala: 'Get your brothers. We are going to visit your grandfather.'

21

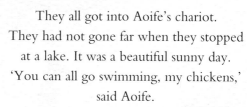

They all got into Aoife's chariot.
They had not gone far when they stopped
at a lake. It was a beautiful sunny day.
'You can all go swimming, my chickens,'
said Aoife.
Fionnuala was worried.
Why was Aoife being nice? She was never nice.
'Stop!' she called to her brothers.
'Don't go into the water!'

But it was too late. Aodh was already swimming
to the middle of the lake. Conn and Fiachra were
splashing each other wildly. Fionnuala went to
the water's edge and called to her brothers again.

But Aoife waved her wand and cast a spell over the children.
Fionnuala began to feel very strange. She could see feathers
sprouting all over her arms and legs. Her toes became webbed
like a duck's. She looked at her brothers. The same thing was
happening to them. The four children had disappeared.
Instead, there were four swans in the water!
Aoife stood on the bank of the lake, laughing.
'Now you can sing all you like!'

Then she chanted her spell:

'You will be swans for nine hundred years.
The first three hundred years you will spend here.
The next three hundred years you will spend on the North Sea.
the next three hundred years you will spend on the Western Ocean.
Only the sound of a bell will save you
and you will become human again.'

Conn and Fiachra started to cry. Fionnuala wanted to cry too, but she said: 'We will fly to our father and tell him what has happened.'
They told King Lir what Aoife had done and Lir was very angry. He could do magic too, and he changed Aoife into a hideous black crow.
She flew away from the palace, cawing angrily. But Lir could not break the spell on his children. So, every day, he went to the lake, where he sat and listened to them singing. And when he died, they still came to that spot to sing together and remember their father.
At the end of three hundred years, the four swans had to leave.

They flew to the North Sea, where the sea was wild and the waves so high they washed over the swan children when they tried to rest. The wind was icy. Sometimes their feet froze to the rocks. They often huddled together and Fionnuala held her brothers under her wings to try to keep them warm.

At last, three hundred years were over. The swans flew over Ireland to the Western Ocean. In the Western Ocean there were little islands where the swan children could rest on soft grass instead of hard rocks. Inish Glora was their favourite island. They would watch the sun set over the sea and sing quietly together. People in the ships passing by heard them and thought they were listening to mermaids.

One day, when they were out fishing, Fiachra, Conn and Aodh came to Fionnuala. Conn said: 'Something strange is happening on Inish Glora.'

The four swans flew towards the island. There they saw a holy man, and he was building a tiny hut of stones. He sang as he worked. When he had finished, he tied something shiny to the top of the hut. It was a bell. The wind blew and the bell began to ring. The children had never heard anything so lovely. The holy man looked up at the four beautiful swans flying round and round above him.

'Come down, my friends,' he said. 'I have heard you singing. Come down and sing with me.'

t as soon as the four children landed on the island, something
ange happened. Their feathers fell from them. The webs fell
m their toes. Fionnuala looked at her brothers. She saw three
         very old men. She herself was a very old woman.
he holy man looked sadly at them. He knew now, from the
ld stories, that they were the Children of Lir, and that they
re going to die. But Fionnuala smiled and said: 'Don't be sad.
Ve are very tired. We have lived very long lives – too long.
Ve'll be happy to sleep here on your island.' The holy man
aptised the four children. Then they lay down on the soft
een grass beside the little hut. And all the birds of the island
              came to sing them to sleep.

THE KING WITH THE DONKEY'S EARS

PRONUNCIATION GUIDE
Donal: *doh-null*; Labhraí: *lowry*;
Loingseach: *leenshock*

There was once a young boy called Donal, who wanted to be a barber. His mother wasn't happy about it. Donal was her only son, and she wanted him to be a famous hero. But Donal didn't want to be a hero. He wanted to cut people's hair and make them look good.

Now, the king of the country, Labhraí Loingseach, had a secret. It was a very big secret. He had donkey's ears. He wore them flattened down under his crown so no one could see them. Whenever he got his hair cut, he had the barber executed immediately afterwards, so his secret would not get out.

Everyone wondered what the big secret was.

One day, Donal was called to the palace to cut the king's ha
His mother threw a terrible fit and refused to let him go. Inst
she herself went to the palace gates and wept and roared an
screamed and bawled. All the courtiers had to go around wi
their fingers in their ears so they wouldn't hear the awful noi
The king couldn't put his fingers
in his ears, because of his secret.
He said: 'What is that woman yowling about?'
The Chief Minister took his fingers out of his ears and said
'What?' The king repeated the question.
'It's her son, the barber,' said the Chief Minister. 'She doesn
want him put to death. She says she won't stop until he is spa
And if he is killed, she says she'll carry on forever!'

at was an awful threat. Labhraí was already so tired of listening
the commotion that he said: 'Very well! I will let her son live.
But he must swear that he will tell nobody what he sees
when he cuts my hair.

Not a word to anything with ears or a mouth.'
And Donal promised. He cut the king's hair.
He saw the king's secret.

Afterwards, Donal found he could think of nothing
but the king's ears. Every time he saw a donkey, he
started guiltily. Every night, he dreamt about ears.
He became pale and sick.

His mother said: 'What's wrong with you now, son?'

'It's the king's secret,' said Donal. 'I'm the only one
in the whole world who knows it.

Not telling anyone is driving me mad.'

'You could tell me,' his mother suggested.

nal knew that if he told his mother the secret, it would be all over the kingdom in about an hour. He shook his head.

'I have sworn not to tell anyone or anything with a mouth or ears.'

s mother sniffed. 'If that's the case,' she said, 'tell something that doesn't have a mouth or ears. Tell a plant or a tree.'

Donal went straight down to the river bank and whispered the king's secret to a big willow tree there.

Afterwards, he felt much better.

But that is not the end of the story. The willow was a lovely
   One day a harper passed by and saw how good the wood w
He needed a new harp, so he cut a branch from the tree and r
one. Then he continued on his way and, as chance would hav
   he was called to play for the court of King Labhraí Loingsea
As soon as he struck his harp it began to sing – all by itself! It s

'Labhraí Loingseach has donkey's ears,
Labhraí Loingseach has donkey's ears,
Labhraí Loingseach has donkey's ears …'

And while the court stared at the king in amazement, the singing went on and on and on. Labhraí was furious. He leapt from his throne. His crown fell off. And his ears, long and pointed and covered in soft fur, could be plainly seen. Everyone could see them. Labhraí Loingseach discovered two things. The first thing he learned was that it is impossible to keep a secret in Ireland. The second thing he learned was that having donkey's ears was not really such a big deal. Life was easier, now that everyone knew his secret. He no longer had to worry all the time about being found out.

For Donal, he had saved all the barbers of the kingdom from certain death. He was a hero. His mother was delighted. And he was made Royal Hairdresser, and was allowed to give the king a much nicer haircut. So he was delighted too!

FIONN AND THE GIANT

PRONUNCIATION GUIDE
Fionn: *fyun*

Bang, bang bang. The door of Fionn's house rattled and shook and then fell down. Standing in the doorway was a big, fat, hairy giant. He had red whiskers and a red nose.

He was wearing red tartan trousers.

Fionn's wife was at home. She was cross with the giant. She had liked her front door.

And now it was gone.

But the giant was five times bigger than she was.

So she said: 'Would you like to come in?'

The giant roared: 'I'm here to fight Fionn! I have made a pathway all the way across the sea from Scotland to come and fight him!'

'Is that right?' said Fionn's wife. 'Sorry, but he's out hunting. Would you like a cup of tea while you're waiting for him?'

The giant was so surprised that he forgot to roar.

He had fought lots of people.

Nobody had ever given him tea.

He said: 'Yes. Do you have cake?'

'I might have,' said Fionn's wife.

'Sit down there by the fire, now.'

The giant sat on the cat and made it yowl.

He did not say sorry.

Fionn's wife made tea. She took out her nicest
cake and she gave it to the giant.

The giant did not say thank you. He put the
whole cake in his mouth. He dribbled crumbs
everywhere. When he had finished the tea and
the cake, he gave a big belch.

'Lovely,' said Fionn's wife. Then she warned:

'Be careful. You might wake the baby.'

'What baby?' said the giant.

Fionn's wife showed him a crib. There was someone asleep i

'That's the baby?' asked the giant.

'It is,' said Fionn's wife.

'But it must be two metres tall,' said the giant.

'Two and a half metres,' said Fionn's wife proudly.

'He has hair all over his face,' said the giant.

'Yes. I have to shave him every day,' said Fionn's wife.

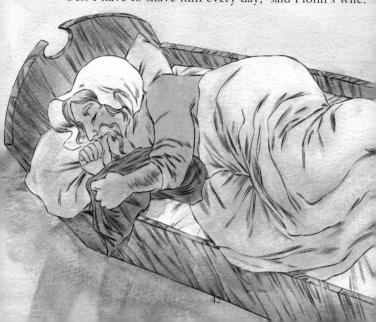

'He looks like he could kill a boar,' said the giant.
'Two this month, already,' said Fionn's wife, smiling,
'with his bare hands.'
'How old is he?' asked the giant.
'He's a month old,' said Fionn's wife, and she looked
fondly at him. The baby opened its eyes and smiled.
'Holy Moley!' said the giant. 'He has an awful set of
teeth in his head.'
'He has, hasn't he?' said Fionn's wife.
The giant was starting to look scared. If Fionn's baby
is this big, he thought, Fionn must be HUGE.
He began to wonder if fighting Fionn was a
good idea.

The baby started to cry. The crying got louder and louder.
It shook the windows of the cottage.
It shook the walls of the cottage.
It would have shaken the door of the cottage, but there was no
door to shake. The giant had knocked it down.
The giant put his fingers in his ears.
Fionn's wife went to a pot on the stove.
She took out a huge bone.
'Give that to the baby, will you?' she said.
The giant tried to put the bone in the baby's mouth. The baby
bit the giant's finger so hard that the giant started to roar.
'Isn't he a little pet?' said Fionn's wife.

'I have just remembered something,' said the giant.
'I have to be home for my dinner. It's haggis tonight!'
He ran out the door. He ran all the way back to Scotland.
stop Fionn following him, he ripped up the path of stones as
he went. The bit that is left is called the Giant's Causeway.
When he got to his house, the giant banged on the door so
hard it fell down. His wife was cross with him.

Fionn's wife wasn't cross any more.

'You can get out of bed now,' she said. 'He's gone.
Our trick worked.'

The big hairy baby in the bed smiled. It was Fionn.

THE WHITE WOLFHOUND

PRONUNCIATION GUIDE
Fionn: *fyun*; Tuiren: *tooren*; Bran: *bran*;
Sceolan: *skiolun*

Fionn had a sister called Tuiren, who was so kind that
everyone loved her. Everyone, that is, except a witch
called Ukdelv, who was jealous of Tuiren's kindness
and loveliness and long fair hair. So, one day, Ukdelv
went to Tuiren's palace, and, waving her magic hazel
wand, she turned the princess into an Irish
wolfhound. But because Tuiren had been fair-haired
and beautiful, the hound was beautiful too,
and its coat was as white as snow.
Ukdelv took Tuiren by the scruff of her neck
and dragged her to the house of a very
grumpy man called Fergus.

Fergus really hated dogs. When he saw Ukdelv
and the big white wolfhound coming towards his
house, he ran outside and barred the door.
'That dog can't come in here,' he said to Ukdelv.
'She's smelly and dirty and she'll drop
hairs everywhere.'
Tuiren looked at him sadly and tried to
lick his hand. He pushed her away.
'Get off me, you big hairy dribbler,' he said.

'But Fionn wants you to take this dog in,'
said Ukdelv. She was sure that Tuiren would
have a terrible life in Fergus's care.
Now, everyone did as Fionn asked, so, with a sigh,
Fergus took the dog into his house. Ukdelv
smiled as she watched Tuiren follow him inside
with her tail tucked between her legs
and her ears down.

But, although the witch had been able to change Tuiren's shape, she could not change her nature. Every time Tuiren saw Fergus, she would try to lick him. She tripped him up with balls, begging to play. She pined when he wasn't there. She was also the best hunting dog in the country, and the two of them spent many happy days together out in the woods and the mountains and the marshes.

So, as time went on, Fergus grew very fond of
Tuiren. 'That dog is nearly human!' he would tell
his friends, not realising that that was exactly
what she was! He called her Princess, not
realising that that was what she really was, too.

He was delighted when she had two little
puppies, which he called Bran and Sceolan. They
would roll around on the floor in front of the fire,
and Fergus would find himself laughing at them.
He sometimes thought Tuiren looked as if
she were laughing too.

Fergus's life was much happier because of Tuiren.
He was no longer grumpy.

But Fionn missed his sister and was afraid that
something bad had happened to her. He used his
magic thumb to discover that she was in Fergus's
house. He travelled there, and as soon as he saw
the big white dog, he knew that it was Tuiren.

She ran to Fionn and put her paws on his
shoulders, licking him all over his face.

Fergus explained how he had got the dog. They
quickly realised that Ukdelv had put a spell on
Tuiren. Together they went to the witch's house
and forced her to turn Tuiren back into a woman.
Fergus was very sad to lose his faithful friend,
but Fionn got him a new puppy for company.
Bran and Sceolan became Fionn's faithful
hunting dogs and stayed with him always.

As for Tuiren, she was very happy to be back with her family and friends in the palace. But because of her time as a dog, she had changed. She sometimes got over-excited when someone mentioned going for a walk. At dinner, there were times when she really, really wanted to pick up the bones from her plate and chew them by the fire. She missed running after rabbits. She missed rolling on her back in the long grass. She missed being able to scratch behind her ear with her foot. She missed being able to lick people she liked and bite people she didn't.

And there were summer evenings when Fionn
would come upon her sitting on the grass outside
the palace, gazing into the sinking sun and
sniffing the wind, as if waiting for someone to
call her home.

OISÍN

PRONUNCIATION GUIDE
Oisín: *usheen*; Niamh: *neev*;
Tír na nÓg: *teer nuh nogue*

56

Oisín was Fionn's son, one of the bravest of the
warriors of the Fianna. He was a poet too, and he
loved to sit looking at the sea or the mountains,
dreaming of faraway things. One day, as he was
sitting by Loch Léin, near Killarney, he saw a
beautiful girl with long golden hair and eyes the
colour of emeralds coming towards him on
a white horse. She was smiling.

'I am Niamh,' she said when she reached him. 'I am
the princess of Tír na nÓg, the Land of the Ever
Young, where there is no sickness or age or death.
I have fallen in love with you, Oisín. Come home
with me and I will make you the happiest man alive.
Climb up onto Moonshadow, and I will take you to
Tír na nÓg.'

So he did. They rode Moonshadow over the hills and
under the waves until they came to Niamh's kingdom.
Oisín was happy in Tír na nÓg. Niamh was as kind as
she was lovely. And Tír na nÓg was a beautiful land.
It was always summer there and no one was ever sad.
But after a while, Oisín began to miss his family and his
friends. He missed Ireland itself, the hills and the lakes
and the rivers of home. Niamh saw that he was
unhappy and asked him what was wrong.

'Let me go home,' said Oisín, 'just for a visit. Just
to see everyone and say goodbye properly. Come
with me. I want you to meet my people.'
Niamh shook her head. She said: 'I cannot go,
and I wish you would not go either. But I
can see your heart is set on it. I will lend you
Moonshadow and he will bring you safely back
to me. But there is one thing you must
remember. You must not put your foot on Irish
ground. Will you promise me that?'

Oisín promised, and kissed his beloved Niamh goodbye.
She watched him go, her emerald eyes full of tears.
Moonshadow carried Oisín over hills and under waves
until they reached Loch Léin. Oisín was back home. But
how different it was! The great palaces were gone and
even the people looked different. They were smaller and
scrawnier and did not seem very happy.

Oisín asked some men, who were trying to lift a big
stone, where he might find Fionn and the rest of the
Fianna. The men looked puzzled. Then an old, white-
haired man, standing nearby, said: 'Oh, I have heard of
the Fianna. Men like giants. But they have all been dead
for hundreds of years.' Oisín gasped. What had seemed
only three years in Tír na nÓg was three hundred in
Ireland! All his friends and all his family were gone. He
would never see them again. Then one of the men said:
'You are a fine, tall fellow, like the heroes of old. Can
you help us lift this rock?'

Oisín leaned down from the back of Moonshadow and pus...
the rock. The rock shifted and fell; but so did Oisín. And as ...
as he touched the ground of Ireland, he became a very old m...
Moonshadow reared up and galloped away. Oisín watched a...
disappeared over the horizon. He knew then that he would n...
be able to return to Tír na nÓg.

Oisín was very sad, and he knew that Niamh would be sad t...

But something good came out of it. Oisín became a famous
storyteller, travelling all over Ireland telling his tales.
It is only because of his stories that we have not forgotten
Fionn and the Fianna, and the heroes and heroines
who lived in Ireland long, long ago.

Originally published 2009 in large format by
The O'Brien Press Ltd.,
12 Terenure Road East, Rathgar, Dublin 6, D06 HD27,
Ireland.
Tel: +353 1 4923333; Fax: +353 1 4922777
E-mail: books@obrien.ie; Website: www.obrien.ie
This edition first published 2011 by The O'Brien Press Ltd
Reprinted 2012, 2013, 2014, 2015, 2017.

ISBN: 978-1-84717-237-2

11 10 9 8
19 18 17

Typesetting, layout, editing, design: The O'Brien Press Ltd
Printed and bound by Factor Druk www.factor-druk.eu..
The paper in this book is produced using
pulp from managed forests.

The O'Brien Press receives assistance from